Someone
Take
the Wheel

By Joe Dolsen

Kill the Middleman Press
2017

Printed and distributed by Kill the Middleman Press.
First paperback edition, First printing: Summer 2017.

Cover photo taken by the author.

Kill the Middleman Press doesn't care what you think
until after you've read the book; it's about the
writing, not the vehicle or the publisher. We strive to
be to writing what independent labels are to punk
rock.

Silas

He held his new driver's license under his nose, inhaled deeply, and pressed its flat rigidness into his skin, absorbing its newly laminated warmth. It had just been spit from whatever machine makes driver's licenses. He drew its melted-plastic fumes into his nostrils and closed his eyes.

His mother looked up from rummaging through her knock-off purse. "What exactly are you doing?" she asked.

He removed the plastic card from his face and looked around the testing facility. Relieved that no one had seen him, he turned back to his mother.

"Here you go," she said as she handed him a Spiderman keychain with two silver keys attached.

"What's this?" he asked, examining the keys.

"I thought it'd be a nice gift. You know, a sort of congratulations for getting your license. It's just a copy of the keys to my car," she said. "I know you wanted your own car, but it's just not in the budget."

He saw a cloud of disappointment dampen her eyes, and he felt guilty. He managed to smile. "That's very thoughtful of you," he said.

He fished his wallet from his back pocket and carefully placed the license behind the clear plastic wallet window.

"Shall we go?" she asked, and without waiting for a response hurried toward the exit. He saw how her shoulders slouched on her slight frame, and how she stared down at the tile floor as she walked. He quickly caught up to her with his long teenage strides. He slipped his arm over her shoulders and squeezed her close. "You do know that I haven't really been into Spiderman since I was ten, right?" he teased.

She smiled, leaned her head into him and slid her arm around his skinny frame. "I know," she said, "but to me, you'll always be that little boy shooting fake spider webs at everyone."

Silas folded himself into the driver's seat and fidgeted his new key copy into the ignition. The Spiderman keychain swung in circles as it dangled from the steering column. He leaned over and fiddled with the tuner until he found his favorite station. As soon as his mom shut her door, he checked all of the appropriate windows and mirrors, put on his seat belt, and cautiously pulled away. Finally, he was a licensed driver who was actually driving.

Ten uneventful minutes later, Silas slowed the car to a stop at the intersection in front of his old elementary school, three blocks from home. A sense of pride rushed over him. *Look how far I've come,* he thought.

The school intersection was hectic. There were parents lined up at the intersection riding high above the world in their SUVs. Every car at the intersection was trying to turn onto the full street to get into the turnaround, trying to pick up their kid. The soccer moms were forgoing their right-of-way at the stop sign, frantically waving to the other drivers at the intersection to go instead of them. Cars were backed up down the block. People were honking. Silas felt the intersection's chaos creep into his body through his eyes, and the sounds forced their way into his ears, resonating deep inside his skull. His hands instantly became sweaty. He felt his heart bouncing below his neck. His ears were smoldering red with anxiety.

"What ever happened to riding the bus?" his mom asked. "This intersection never used to be this crazy."

The crossing guard, armed with her portable stop sign, seemed oblivious to the pandemonium around her. She guided the little kids and their matching parent across the street. There were minivans lurching into the street from parking spots, forcing their way into the bumper-to-bumper traffic. Silas pulled the car up to the crosswalk. He watched as the crossing guard guided eight little kids, like rambunctious ducklings, in front of his car.

"Mom?" Silas exhaled, panic in his voice.

"What, Silas?" his mom asked, concerned.

"What if my foot accidentally slips from the brake?" His knuckles whitened as he vocalized the thought.

"Silas, that's not funny," his mom said. She leaned forward and punched the power button, shutting off the radio; there was a popping sound in the speakers, and then silence. She looked at the kids and then looked at Silas's foot on the brake pedal. His leg was locked at the knee, and he was pressing the pedal to the floor so hard that his foot *was* slipping sideways off of the brake. "Ease up on the brake," she advised.

"I'm afraid to. The car'll lurch into those kids. Oh my god, I don't want to hurt those little kids." The sound of Silas's shallow breathing filled the car.

"Silas, you *need* to calm down," his mom snapped. She pulled the emergency brake between them as hard as she could.

"Is it my turn... to go? Is it my turn yet?" Silas asked, not realizing what his mother had just done. He struggled to make sense of the intersection.

"Silas, put the car in park and switch seats with me," she commanded. "The emergency brake is on." He sat there, paralyzed. "Just do it," she yelled. She waited with her hand on the door handle, ready to jump out and run over to the driver's side the minute he put it in park. He slowly uncoiled his fingers from the steering wheel and put the car in park. His mother leaped from the car and bolted across the front of the car to the driver's side door, startling the crossing guard in the process. "Get out! Get out of the car. I'm driving!" she said as she flung Silas's door open.

Silas obeyed and skittishly skirted around the back of the car. He dropped, defeated, into the passenger seat and pulled the door shut behind him.

They sat in stifling silence until they got home. Silas's mom pulled into the parking garage, put the car in park, and sat there with the engine running. Silas popped his door open. "I'm sorry," he said. "I don't know what came over me. I panicked," he said before he exited the car.

She nodded her head and without looking at him said, "I'm just going to take a few minutes here, if you don't mind." Silas got out, walked to the back stoop of their building and watched as she sat there. He watched her shut the car off. He watched her pull the keys from the ignition, and he watched her stare at the Spiderman keychain lying in the palm of her small hand. He wondered what she was thinking. *She's probably wishing that I was ten again*, he thought. *I wish I was ten again.*

Chloe

"What the fuck!" Chloe yelled at the icy blue eyeball peeking through the keyhole, watching her on the toilet. Her long, earthy skirt fell to her ankles as she lunged toward the door. She tripped over her underwear that had been pulled down to her ankles. "You little pervert!" she hollered from the dirty tile floor. She listened as the little footsteps scuttled down the hallway and out the back door. She had no way of knowing exactly which cousin had been spying on her, there were so many of them.

Nine people in all lived in her uncle and aunt's four-bedroom house, no basement. She shared a bedroom with the youngest three boys who, thankfully, hadn't reached puberty yet. She hadn't been there long enough to know which boys were blood relatives and which were foster kids that her aunt took in for extra cash; she didn't really care, either.

She stood and pulled up her skirt and underwear, and then aligned them. Then she reflexively felt her pocket for the pregnancy test she had stolen from Walgreens earlier that afternoon. *Still there*. She was pretty sure she was pregnant. She was sure because, ever since her first period, she'd been super regular, and from the start she'd counted the number of eggs she'd passed through her body: fifty-five so far. She really should've passed number fifty-six by now, maybe even number fifty-seven. She figured she was over a month pregnant.

She walked through the house, across the worn carpet that had once been thick brown shag. She looked for somewhere to take the test, but every room was either occupied or not private enough. She finally stepped outside and maneuvered the door back into its lopsided frame as she pulled it shut. She took a moment to inhale the bright sunshine. She liked how the sun's high noon light darkened the edges of the green trees around her, making everything look crisp. She looked to the sun, shut her eyes, and held her arms out straight; the sun's rays penetrated her skin and warmed her down to her bones and joints.

The thought of the pregnancy test in her pocket snapped her out of her heat-induced trance.

She crunched across the dead brown grass to the side door of the garage. At first, she wasn't able to open it. She leaned her body against it and pushed with all her might. The door reluctantly gave way with a dull scraping sound coming from the other side. She pushed the door open just enough to quickly slip inside. The garage had not been used in years; it was packed shoulder high with junk from back to front.

She found an empty five-gallon bucket flecked with concrete, and halfheartedly tried to brush it clean. She gave up and set it down. She started throwing objects on top of the high pile of bric-a-brac, clearing a little space for herself. She placed the bucket in the middle of the clearing and dug around in her pocket for the pregnancy test. She un-wrapped it and threw the litter on top of the junk pile. She didn't bother reading the directions; she knew the drill. She hiked up her skirt, pulled down her underwear, and squat-hovered over the five-gallon bucket. She began to pee. She skillfully held the test midstream and prayed that she wasn't pregnant, that her near two-month lack of ovulation was due to the stress involved in moving from her mom's apartment, which was downstate Illinois, to her aunt's house just outside of Chicago. As she prayed, she heard her urine splatter heavily against the bottom of the green plastic pail; the deep echo escaped the bucket from between her legs.

Chloe carefully set the test on a junk ledge and pulled up her underwear and skirt, straightened and smoothed out her long skirt, took the wire handle of the bucket in one hand, and cautiously climbed to the top of the junk pile. She dumped the urine on the pile of junk. She jumped backward, landing on her feet. She listened as the liquid trickled down through the discarded cans, old chairs, green plastic milk crates full of rusted pipes and tools, and black plastic bags. It dripped like a leaky roof, all the way down to the concrete floor. She flipped the bucket upside down, sat, and waited for the results. She held the stick in her hand and watched as a blue test line gradually turned into an addition symbol. The change was so subtle that she had to close her eyes, regroup, and then take another look. "Yup, it's positive," she said.

She inhaled deeply, dropped her head into her hands, and started to cry until she realized that the urine-saturated test stick was still in her hand and was dangerously close to her curly hair. She felt so lonely. She wanted to tell someone, but knew that telling her mom would only make things worse, and she would never dream of telling her aunt. She didn't know if she'd be welcome to stay or not.

She sat straight up when she heard something rustling around outside the garage. "Fucking pervert cousins," she said under her breath. She panicked; thinking that one of them would stumble across the pregnancy test, or the discarded box, and tell her aunt. She climbed up on the bucket; careful not to touch the urine-saturated area, and collected the test box and wrapper, dropped the stick back into the box, and slipped it into her skirt pocket. She found a small gardening shovel hanging on the garage wall, took it, and held it inconspicuously at her side.

Chloe stepped out of the garage and waited a beat while her eyes adjusted to the sunlight. She made sure she wasn't being watched and hurried around to the back of the garage and then ducked under the cover of a pine tree, fell to her knees, and began to dig as quickly as she could. The soil under the tree was loose. A damp-earth smell filled her nostrils as she turned the soil with the shovel. As soon as the hole was deep enough, she pulled the box from her pocket and pushed it deep into the rich soil, crushing the box with her dirty fingers. With both hands, she reached out and pulled the loose soil pile toward her, filling the hole. She stood and stomped the loose earth down and kicked brown pine needles over the fresh earth scar. She threw the shovel further under the tree, brushed her hands against her skirt, and walked to the house, scanning the windows and shadows for subzero blue eyes housed in meddlesome little faces.

That night she slept restlessly. She dreamed that the test had grown from the fertile soil into a huge tree with brown-edged orange bark. Instead of leaves, she saw each and every one of her four hundred remaining eggs hanging from the tree. They looked like shiny Christmas ornaments, only there was a dull, rainbow membrane coating the eggs. She instinctively covered her pelvis with both hands and wondered how they got from her ovaries to the tree. She smelled rain in the air and felt full gray clouds surround her waist; they gently squeezed her belly. Then she heard hundreds of babies cry in unison. Their cries sounded plastic, like they came from toy babies. Through the thick clouds she felt for the tree. She wanted to help the babies, but she couldn't find the tree trunk. She kept walking. The crying grew louder and more intense. It sounded less toy-ish and more real with every step she took.

She sat straight up in bed, wide awake, looked to the light coming in from the open door across the room, and became aware of her aunt's presence. She was sitting on one of the boy's beds, comforting him.

"Is everything all right?" Chloe asked.

"Your screaming woke him up," her aunt's silhouette said. Chloe could just barely make out her aunt's fingers running through her cousin's hair.

"I'm sorry. I had a bad dream," she said. At that moment, she longed for her mom to be sitting next to her, stroking her hair, but she wasn't. This is where she was sent to live. This was her new home.

Silas

"Silas, I've got a letter for you… It's from your father," his mother called in a singsongy manner from the front hallway. He knew she'd been drinking. He could hear it in her voice. Seconds later there was a thud against his bedroom door and then she stumble-spilled into his room.

"What cha doin?" she asked as she opened the door.

Silas just stood there. She grabbed his chin and turned his face to hers. "What do I see in those eyes of yours?" she asked, rocking his face back and forth. Her pierce penetrated his pupils. He flinched. She pushed his face away.

"I feel sorry for you," he said.

"Why?"

Silas shrugged.

"You think I'm a drunk, don't you? Cause that's what it seems like."

"Can I please just have my letter?" he asked.

She looked at the envelope in her hand as if she'd forgotten it was there. "Sure," she said, handing it over to him.

He wanted her to leave his bedroom before he opened the letter. He flipped it around in his hands, pretending to examine every detail of the envelope, hoping that she'd get bored with his dawdling and leave.

"Well, aren't you going to open it?" she asked. He could smell the sourness of the red wine on her breath. He sat on his bed and opened the letter:

Dear Silas,
A little birdie told me that you got your license.
Congratulations! I'm so proud of the man you're
becoming! I want to show you how proud I am, so
I've enclosed a check for $5,000 for you to buy a
decent used car. The only stipulation I'm putting on
this is that the car has to be dependable enough for
you to drive up to Minnesota and visit me the first
break you get from school. My advice would be that
you choose dependability over flash; it will make you
happier in the long run. Again, I am very proud of
you, and am proud of the man you're becoming. I
love you.
Love,
Dad

"Well?" his mom asked.

"Well, what?"

"What'd he say?"

"He said he was proud of me for getting my license," Silas said, quickly forcing the letter back into the envelope, not wanting her to see the check.

"Bullshit. That's not all," she said, snatching the envelope from Silas.

"Mom!" he protested. "That's mine." She turned her back to him and pulled out the letter and check.

She read the letter, looked at the check, and threw it back at him. "I bust my ass every day to make sure you have good food and nice clothes, and he thinks he can just swoop down and buy your love?"

"Jesus, Mom. You make it sound like my love is for sale, or something. Give me a break. He's my *fucking* dad..." As soon as the words left his mouth, Silas's mom slapped him. His face stung. He felt unwelcome tears rush to his eyes.

Chloe

The screaming baby tree relentlessly haunted Chloe's dreams. Her eggs were hanging higher, farther and farther out of reach. Winds drove debris into the hanging eggs. Silver pods of potential burst into nothing, leaving goops of glowing gray yolk on the forest floor, flecked with gritty ground dust. Every night, over and over, the crying babies hung there in the ever expanding tree. They hung in the fog. She couldn't save them. She couldn't find them, but she could hear them crying.

The dreams happened so often that Chloe began thinking of them as fertility nightmares. She would wake up, fearing that she had revealed her secret to her aunt, who, more often than not, would be sitting across the dark room, stroking her son's hair. At those moments, Chloe wanted to slip back into her nightmares, where she knew things were bad, but at least they weren't real.

"You're going to have to get a grip on yourself," her aunt's voice cut like a knife through the darkness. Chloe could hear the anger in her aunt's whispers. It always felt like a veiled threat, like an unfinished sentence, like the next part would go something like, *or you're going to have to find somewhere else to live.*

Chloe hated the havoc the unborn baby in her belly brought. She was tired all the time. She didn't sleep. She would wake to her own screams. She would stare at the ceiling and count the anxiety-fueled beats of her hammering heart. Everything echoed eternally in her head. She watched the lights of the passing cars glide across the ceiling, and she would think about dying.

She thought about stealing sleeping pills from her aunt and washing them down with white wine while she sat in a warm bathtub. She knew it would be peaceful, sleeping to death. She didn't want to do this alone. She wanted to die.

She would have to be fully clothed though, so her perverted cousins wouldn't find her naked body.

Silas

Evening shadows crept into the living room. Silas watched from the hallway as his mother sat in dim silence. She seemed to be in a trance. He wondered what ghosts were floating through her head. He walked in, reached up under the yellowed lampshade, and pulled the ball chain, lighting the room.

His mom snapped to attention at the light. "Oh, hey, I didn't see you there," she said.

"Yeah. Hey. I'm going to a party tonight."

"Have a good time and down one for me, then."

"Stop being so sarcastic. It's ugly. Besides, I don't drink," Silas reminded her.

"Famous last words," she said and smiled as she took a sip. "Where's this party at, anyway?"

"At some girl's house."

"Is it going to be supervised?"

"Honestly, I don't think so," Silas said, fishing in his pocket for his car keys.

"Okay, have a good time." She waved her hand behind her head as she picked up the remote and turned on the television.

Silas snorted.

"Why the snort?" she asked, flipping through channels.

"Well, you asked all the right questions… You made it sound like you care, but you didn't bat an eyelash when I told you that the girl's parents wouldn't be there."

His mom put down her wine, swiveled her chair around, slapped her thighs with both hands, and said, "Oh no! Her parents aren't going to be there? Well you'd better stay home and not involve yourself in such debauchery." She raised both hands to her cheeks and opened her mouth, feigning shock. "There, is that good enough for ya? Now do I get my mom of the year award back?" She turned to the TV, picked up her wine, and leaned back in the chair.

"I'll see you in the morning," Silas mumbled under his breath as he walked to the door.

"Don't come home with a venereal disease," she called after him and again raised her glass to the air.

Chloe

The tiny house turned into a pressure cooker when the summer sun beat down on its black roof; her aunt's refusal to turn on the air conditioner simply made matters worse. The warm air in the house smelled like dirty diapers and rotten guacamole. Chloe's aunt had neglected everything but the basics, the things she had to do, like feed the kids and change their diapers. She seemed depressed, and her uncle was nowhere to be found.

The stench haunting the house forced Chloe out for a walk. The hot summer air blew her skirt and long curly hair behind her as she shut her eyes and walked blindly into the breeze. She imagined that she was a bird soaring high in the sky until she panicked and felt the sudden need to open her eyes. When she did, she heard high-pitched laughter ricocheting off of the neighborhood homes. She saw a playground filled with kids climbing monkey-bars mountain and kids soaring high on swings, their feet trying to kick holes in the sky.

She was drawn to the park like a fly to sugar water. She walked over, sat down on a bench, and watched the kids play. She watched the mothers perched on their benches, leaning toward each other, their hands conducting invisible conversations. She envied their bulky baby bags emblazoned with bold colors and wild patterns. *I could never have that,* she thought. *I don't deserve that.* She began nervously biting her fingernails.

There was a little girl dressed in a puffy pink shirt and yellow, diaper-padded shorts. The girl had clambered up onto a swing and sat there, waiting for it to go. Chloe watched. "Mama, mama!" the girl called. The girl's mother was so engrossed in conversation that she didn't hear the little voice calling over the playground commotion. Chloe got up and walked over to the little girl.

"Do you want me to push you?" she asked. The little girl's eyes followed Chloe as she walked behind the swing. Chloe gently pushed the swing seat.

"No! No! Mama! Mama!" the girl yelled, panicking. The mother ran over.

"Is everything okay, sweetheart?" she asked as she scooped her daughter up from the swing and hurried back toward the bench. She examined her daughter as she went. Chloe stood there, dumbfounded.

"I was just trying to help," Chloe called after them.

"Thanks, but we're fine," the mom yelled back over her shoulder. The other mothers stopped what they were doing and stared at Chloe.

"Yeah, well, maybe you should pay a little more attention to your kid," Chloe called after her.

Chloe walked away. Tears streamed down her face. She didn't bother wiping them away, just let them flow. She watched as they crashed to the sidewalk where they were quickly absorbed by the porous concrete and imagined that the sun peeled her trail of tears from the sidewalk, each tear evaporating into the summer air, like they never even existed at all.

Silas

Silas and Eric drove toward the scarlet summer sunset with their windows down and the music loud. The warm wind danced in and out of the car, grazing their faces, kissing their cheeks, tickling their ears, whispering, *you are invincible, you are indomitable, you are indestructible,* filling their heads with the evening's endless possibilities. They pulled up to a stop sign and an older couple crossed in front of Silas's car.

"You know, it sort of freaks me out when people walk in front of my car," he said.

"Really? Why?" Eric asked.

"I don't know. I'm afraid my foot's going to slip off of the brake onto the accelerator and I'm going to go plowing into them or something."

"Shut the fuck up," Eric said, glancing down at Silas's foot. "Stop fucking with me."

Silas smiled. Eric leaned forward, dashboard lights glowing on his face. He turned the music down. "You know, Bree's supposed to be there, right?"

"Really?" Silas asked and glanced at Eric for reassurance.

"Yes really. I guess she was asking if you were going to be there," Eric said, looking straight ahead, making it difficult for Silas to get a read on him.

"Are you messing with me?" Silas asked.

"No. I'm legit," Eric said, still looking straight ahead.

"Holy shit! Really?" Silas asked.

"No. I'm just busting your balls. She wasn't asking about you, but she *is* supposed to be there."

"You piece of shit," Silas said and thumped Eric across the chest with the back of his hand.

Silas parked the car. The cars lining the street looked out of place in the quiet neighborhood, and the small groups of high school kids migrating from the cars to the party house begged for a concerned neighbor to call the police. Eric and Silas walked up the sidewalk, Eric with his brown bag of bottled beer clinking with every step. There was a line of high schoolers waiting to get inside. They slowly made their way in line to an immense guy sitting on a stool just inside the doorway.

"Five dollars for a cup," the muscled mass said.

"It's cool. Don't need a cup. Brought our own," Eric said as he hoisted the brown bag to his chest.

"Like I said, five dollars for a cup. I could give a shit what you put in it," the guy said as he stepped off of his stool and filled the entrance.

"Do you have any money?" Eric asked; his voice leaped an octave as he frantically dug through his pockets.

"I've got a twenty," Silas said.

"That'll do," the door guy said and snatched it from Silas's hand.

"What about change?" Eric asked.

"I don't believe in change," the guy mumbled under his breath and turned to collect money from the entwined couple standing behind Eric and Silas.

"I just saw him with a wad of cash," Eric said, looking back at the money guy. Silas put his hands on Eric's shoulders and steered him into the party.

Silas froze when he saw the state of disrepair in the living room. *This is not my house. This is not my problem. I am not responsible for this mess,* he said to himself. The curtains that had once hung over the windows were yanked down and precariously perched at odd angles in the deep window frames. The off-white carpet was stained, from wall to wall, with beer spills. Silas thought it looked like a dog had pissed all over the floor, marking his territory. People were smoking joints and cigarettes and just flicking their ashes on the carpet. The resulting black holes released a burnt plastic smell that commingled with the pungent pot tang and filled the room.

Music was pulsating, rippling across the room. Its deep thud drowned out every other sound. The rapidly flashing lights by the DJ's station were under the spell of the music, painting the smoke alternating rainbow colors. Eric said something to Silas.

"I can't hear you!" Silas yelled.

Eric leaned in closer. "Dude, this is fucked up!" he yelled. Silas leaned back to read Eric's face. *Was it a good fucked up or a bad fucked up?* Eric smiled, reached into his crinkled, brown beer bag, and handed Silas a bottle. Silas twisted the lid off of the beer and drank it down.

"Eric, give me another one." Eric looked surprised. "I thought you weren't much of a drinker?"

"Tonight I am." Eric sat the bag down and grabbed two beers. He handed a beer to Silas. He twisted the lid off and gently tossed it at a cute girl dancing with a group of girls. She looked over her shoulder. He smiled and waved; she smiled, walked over, took his hand, and pulled him over to dance with her group. Eric obliged. He threw his head back and drained the beer. He motioned for Silas to join the group. Silas put his hand up, refusing. Eric knew better than to force the issue. He held up his empty bottle and shook it, wanting another. Silas reached in the bag, twisted off the lid and handed the beer to Eric. Silas decided to check out the rest of the party.

As he turned to leave the living room, he saw Bree dancing with a group of people in the corner. He watched her from a distance. He didn't want to seem creepy, but he loved watching her. He knew that he loved her from the moment he saw her in Spanish class. In class, he would often lean forward in his desk and inhale her vanilla scent. She was perfect. She was a little shorter than most girls in school, but, in Silas's estimation, she had perfect proportions. Some people, mostly other girls, thought she was a bit of a bitch, but Silas thought that was beautiful. He attributed her attitude to her firecracker spirit. He figured she had to be that way to survive, in order to get what she wanted, in order to call her own shots, all things Silas admired.

She saw him and waved. He waved back. She stopped dancing and walked over to him.

"Hi!" Bree yelled, standing on her tiptoes, her hand on his shoulder, trying to reach Silas's ear.

"Hi, Bree," Silas yelled back, leaning down to her, inhaling everything he could, feeling like a bit of a perv.

"Where'd you get the bottled beer?" she asked. "This keg stuff is shit."

"You want one?" Silas asked.

"Sure." Bree smiled and flipped her hair.

"One second," Silas said and hurried off to Eric's brown bag. When he returned, Bree was dancing with her group, mostly made up of guys. Silas tapped on her shoulder. He figured Bree had just used him to get what she wanted, and he blushed as he handed her the bottle. He turned to continue his exploration of the party. He hadn't walked five feet before he felt a tug at the tail of his shirt. He turned to find Bree.

"Thanks," she said.

"Oh, yeah. Sure. No problem," he said.

"You're in my Spanish class, right?" she asked.

"Yeah, I sit behind you," Silas said.

"What?" she said, and stood on her tiptoes, cupping her ear.

"I said, I sit right behind you," Silas said. Her hair brushed his cheek.

"I'm having a hard time hearing you," she said. Silas figured the inability for them to carry on a decent conversation was probably her out, so she could go back to dancing. He stood up straight and nodded, as if he understood what was happening. She grabbed his hand and walked him down the hall. She knocked on a door. No answer. She entered the dark room and shut the door behind them. She pulled Silas across the room and climbed up on the single bed. She patted the space beside her.

"Sit here," she said. "Let's talk." He sat next to her and inhaled deeply, expecting to smell her sweet vanilla scent; to his surprise, he only smelled alcohol and marijuana. She took his arm and put it around her. Silas felt a bulge materializing in his pants.

"How much have you had to drink?" Silas asked. "Are you okay?"

"Kelly and I've been drinking since noon. Been smoking a wee bit of weed, too," she laughed. "I was really fucked up a few hours ago, stoned off of my ass, laughing at everything."

"Oh," Silas said. She nestled into his side.

"Do you smoke?" she asked.

"What? weed?"

"Yeah, weed."

"Never tried it," he said, shifting, trying to adjust.

"Wanna?"

"Sure. I guess." She pulled out a one hitter and a small pink lighter. Silas watched her.

"It's not mine. It's Kelly's. She's so messed up. She doesn't even know I have this." She gave him the one hitter and lit the lighter for him. He inhaled. "The longer you hold it, the better it'll work," she coached. He inhaled deeply and held his breath until he couldn't hold it anymore and had to cough it all out. She laughed. "Try it again," she said and relit the weed. He inhaled, hearing the weed crackle under the influence of the flame. He held it even longer and then laughed it out.

"This stuff is crazy," he said. "I can't feel my arms. I think they might float right up to the ceiling." Bree smiled and reached over him and grabbed two beers. She opened one and gave it to Silas and opened one for herself. Silas slammed his beer and reached for another.

"Whoa, slow down there, tiger," Bree said as Silas cracked the second one open.

"I'm fine," he said. "I got this."

He sat there, his arm around her, not exactly sure what he should do next. He looked at her. He watched her chest rise and fall with each breath she took. His eyes traced the moonlight lines of her breasts as their curves disappeared into her low-cut shirt. He watched her throat as she drank her beer. *I want to kiss her so bad*, he thought, *but I need to wait for that perfect moment. I need to make sure this is what's really happening.* They sat in silence. And more silence.

"Umm, I think I'm going to go to the bathroom," Bree said as she reached over Silas and grabbed another beer. "The line might be long," she said as she scooted her way off of the bed.

"Yeah, of course. I'll be here," he said. She walked out of the room and closed the door behind her.

Silas squinted in the dark. He saw Hello Kitty posters plastered on the walls. The bed had a canopy over it, and there was a huge dollhouse in the corner beside what looked like a gigantic stuffed teddy bear sitting next to it. The room started spinning and he put his beer on the bedside stand, next to a princess clock that glowed in the dark. He crawled under the covers with his shoes still on and shut his eyes, trying to stop the room from spinning.

Silas woke up to Eric shaking him by the shoulders. "Dude, we gotta get outta here," he said. The sun peeked through pink curtains. He looked around the room. He had kicked the yellow bedspread off the bed, and his shoes had left a grimy smear on the girl's yellow bed sheet. He rolled off of the bed and sluggishly followed Eric out of the room. The house looked like a bomb had gone off in the living room and red plastic beer cup shrapnel had exploded everywhere. He felt like he was in a war zone; he carefully stepped over casualties passed out on the floor. His head pounded and his ears buzzed. Silas searched the main room for Bree.

"Hey, Eric…"

"Yeah?"

"Have you seen Bree anywhere?" he asked, squinting, looking around.

"No. No I haven't seen her anywhere. I haven't seen her all night, man. Why do you ask? Did you see something?" Eric spoke quickly.

"No. Relax. I'm just curious," Silas said as he almost tripped over a party casualty.

"I am relaxed. Why wouldn't I be relaxed?" Eric asked. "We gotta get outta here, though. Quick like."

"Fine. Let's go home."

Eric had to drive Silas's car to Silas's mom's apartment and had to pull over twice for Silas to throw up. He had fallen asleep by the time they arrived at the building. With a lot of coaxing and Silas's arm thrown over his shoulder, Eric got Silas up the stairs and into his bedroom. Silas's mom was still asleep. Eric pulled Silas's shoes off and helped him into bed.

"You're a good friend, Eric," Silas said before he passed out and Eric left.

Chloe

Chloe decided to duck into the grocery store on the way home from her library adventure. *Such a waste of my fucking time*, she thought as she walked down the beige tiled grocery aisle. The loud buzzing of the fluorescent overhead lights stopped her in her tracks, and she wondered if being pregnant heightened her senses. She realized that she was hungrier than she had ever remembered being in all of her entire seventeen years on this Earth. She wanted candy.

She looked at the signage hanging from the ceiling for the candy aisle: *Produce*, *Juices*, *Soups*, and then she saw a sign in the corner of the store that caught her eye: *Pharmacy*. She walked over and strolled up and down the pharmacy aisles until she saw the prenatal vitamins right next to the locked prophylactic display case. *That's ironic*, she thought and snorted. *I wish stores didn't feel the need lock these things up*, she thought as she ran her fingers across the display-case glass. *I wouldn't be here now if they didn't.*

She picked up the most expensive prenatal vitamins she could find. *My baby's going to have nothing but the best*, she thought as she tried to make sense of the label. *I can't understand half of this shit,* she thought as she rolled the bottle around in her hand. *Maybe this pregnancy shit is more complicated than I thought.*

She carried the plastic jar of prenatal vitamins to the candy aisle where she picked out three bags of Sour Patch Kids, and, with little more than a casual flick of the wrist, she slipped the candy and the vitamins into her green canvas purse. She turned around quickly only to find a woman glaring at her, her loaded shopping cart parked awkwardly between them.

"I saw what you did," the woman said. Chloe immediately hated her. She hated her brown curly hair and her ugly too-short bangs. She hated her too-tight, acid-washed mom jeans and her pink tank top. Chloe thought she was trying too hard to look young.

"What did you see me do?" Chloe asked.

"Shove all of that stuff into your purse. Without paying for it."

"You need to get your eyes checked, lady," Chloe said, trying to move around the woman's shopping cart.

"I'll wait here until you return the items… Or, I'll call the store manager and follow you around until he comes. I'm sure he'll want to call the police." The woman took her phone out of her tight pants pocket and leaned her arms on the handle of the cart while she searched her smart phone for the store phone number.

"Fine," Chloe said and pulled the prenatal vitamins from her purse. She handed them to the lady rather than put them back on the shelf. *She can put that shit away*. The woman stared at the label and processed what the jar was and what it meant.

"Were these for you?" the woman asked. She looked at Chloe in disbelief.

"Are you happy?" Chloe asked. She pushed past the woman's shopping cart and hurried toward the exit. The minute she got out of the store, she dug deep into her backpack and pulled out the stolen bag of Sour Patch Kids. She ripped the bag open and tossed the plastic wrapping behind her. She dropped three pieces into her mouth, one at a time. She loved wedging the candy against the roof of her mouth and sucking the sugar off of the sour gummy pieces.

As Chloe walked down the sidewalk, she thought about running away. She had done it before. She used to run away from her mom's place all the time. She was addicted to the feeling of freedom that coursed through her body every time she set out on a new adventure. Running away filled her heart with hope. It usually wasn't until the sun set that the reality of not having a place to sleep weighed so heavy on her that her euphoric bubble burst. That's why she liked to run away in the mornings, so she could stretch that runaway elation throughout the entire day.

It was too late to runaway today; besides, she wasn't exactly sure what she would be running from: the baby was inside. The sun peeked through the green of the tall tree's leaves as the branches smoothly swayed in the summer breeze. The cooling of the afternoon weather had almost convinced her that the day wasn't so bad; after all, she had stolen three bags of her favorite candy. She smiled and looked up at the sun. It was at that moment that a blue Volvo station wagon abruptly pulled over, right in front of her. She stopped and stared, dumbfounded. She initially wondered if it was a drive-by, but then figured the car was too suburban. The driver's door opened and out stepped the woman from the grocery store. She waved her hands. "Stop," she yelled, despite the fact that Chloe had already stopped.

Chloe, ready to run, waited and watched as the woman came toward her. *What the hell does she want?* Chloe wondered. *She'd better not touch me.* She clenched her fists at her sides and decided to stand her ground.

"Hey," the woman called as she ambled toward Chloe. "I bought these for you." She held out a plastic bag. The way she held it reminded Chloe of a farmer holding a dead chicken by its neck, its limp body swinging, echoing the woman's movements. Chloe apprehensively snatched the bag from the woman and peeked inside. "It's the vitamins," the woman said, "I figured you needed them. I asked myself, what would Jesus do in this situation? So I bought them, and now, I'm giving them to you… No questions asked. No strings attached." The woman held her hands up, turned, and walked back to her car. Chloe just stood there, speechless. The woman climbed into her car and drove away.

Her face had turned red with embarrassment, which quickly turned to anger. She throttled the neck of the plastic bag and flung it toward the car as it sped off. "Fuck you, bitch. I don't need your pity or your charity." The car disappeared around a corner.

Chloe hurried across the dried grass to where the bag of vitamins had landed. She was crying, but she wasn't sure why. She couldn't figure out exactly what she was feeling, which only frustrated her and compounded her anger. She bent down and dumped the plastic bottle of vitamins out of the gray grocery bag, tossed the plastic bag into the street, and, once again, dropped the vitamins into her purse. She popped three more pieces of candy into her mouth and angrily chewed them. By the time she got to her aunt's house, she had stopped crying and had devoured an entire bag of candy. The roof of her mouth was raw from the sugar granules. The rawness felt good. She felt alive.

Silas and Eric - The Last Drive

Silas concentrated on the black two-lane highway that stretched out before him, buzzing tires below. He loved the freedom his car gave him. He would pick Eric up on Saturdays or Sundays and spend the afternoon listening to music and driving away from the obnoxious suburban sprawl until they reached the wind-burnt cornfields that lined the Illinois highways. They would talk about anything, about everything. Sometimes, they would just sit and listen to music, hypnotized by the ever-changing angles of the corn rows as the car sped across the flat state.

"Hey, there's something I need to tell you before you read it online," Eric said, staring intently at his phone.

"Okay," Silas said. "What's up?"

"Not now. We should probably be stopped for this conversation."

"Just tell me," Silas said.

"No... You should probably pull over," Eric said.

"Huh? Why?" Silas asked, worried now.

"Um, yeah, you're not going to like this conversation," Eric said, still staring at his phone.

Silas exited the highway and pulled into the nearest gas station. He slammed the car into park, throwing Eric forward, his seatbelt catching him, and he snatched the phone from Eric. Eric turned off the radio as Silas read.

Silence.

"What the fuck!" Silas finally yelled. "Tell me this isn't true." He looked at Eric. Eric looked down at his hands. "It's true?"

"Mostly," Eric said, still staring at his hands.

"Did you two go all the way?"

"No... Well, almost…"

"Almost? What's that mean?"

"We didn't have protection."

"Dude! What the fuck? When?"

"At the party."

"You knew I liked her! I can't believe it." Silas pounded the steering wheel with his palm. "The other day, you sat there and let me tell you about hanging out with her on the bed. I told you she left to go to the bathroom and never came back. She was with you?"

"Yeah," Eric said, picking at his thumbnail.

"What kind of friend are you anyway? You're not a friend. I thought we were best friends…"

"Silas, listen…"

"Nothing you can say will make this any better," Silas said and pounded the steering wheel with the palm of his hand over and over.

"I'm really sorry, Silas. I just couldn't believe that a girl like that would like me, plus I'd been drinking. I don't know man, I just wanted her to love me I guess," Eric said and leaned his head against the car window.

"Dude. Fuck you," Silas said and put the car in reverse.

"I'm really sorry, man," Eric said.

"Please, just don't talk to me," Silas looked over his shoulder and backed out of the parking spot.

The ride home was long and silent, except for the radio and the music and the tires hissing on the highway.

Chloe

She opened the backdoor to her aunt's, dropped her backpack to the floor, and plopped down on the dark green couch. Dust particles burst into the low afternoon sunlight. She watched as they danced in the air and wondered how long it would take before they fell to the ground, dirtying everything they fell on. She covered her eyes with the back of her hand and started to drift off.

"Chloe! Is that you?" her aunt yelled from another room.

"Yeah," she hollered back.

"Thank god." She rushed into the room. "I need you to watch the boys for a minute while I run to the store. It's a bit of a womanly emergency, if you know what I mean." She grabbed her car keys from the hook and slowly turned toward Chloe. "I guess you *do* know what I mean, don't you?" She stood there, eyebrows raised. Chloe panicked and nodded, hoping her aunt didn't stop and do the math. "I'm so sorry I didn't think about this before." She disappeared into the kitchen and came back with a pen and a pad of paper. "Write down what you need...you know the specifics, and I'll pick them up for you."

Chloe didn't reach for the pen and paper. She sat there and stared at her aunt holding the pen and paper.

"Oh my god! You're not pregnant, are you?" her aunt asked. She put her hand on her hip, and searched her face.

"No, no, no..." Chloe felt her heart pounding so hard that she feared it was rocking her body back and forth. "I just can't remember what kind I of tampon I used. Mom and I shared, and she usually bought whatever was on sale," Chloe said, not exactly sure where that had come from, but happy it did.

"Figures," her aunt said. "She's such a tight ass."

"I know that a lot of the times the box was blue and green..."

"I'll look for the box, then," she said and slung her purse over her shoulder. "I'll be right back."

When the screen door slammed shut, Chloe leaned back on the couch. She couldn't believe how tired she'd been lately. She drifted off to sleep and dreamt about her new science partner, Silas, only in her dream, he was in her bedroom back home, trying to sell her a box of maxi pads, telling her that tampons were for dirty sluts.

She woke to the deep thud of a car door closing in the driveway. Her aunt hurried in and handed off a bag. "Here you go," she said, as she rushed past her to the bathroom. Chloe pulled the box of tampons from the bag and wondered what she'd do with them. She fought back tears. *Don't cry! There's no reason to cry*, she told herself.

She went to her room and lay down on her mattress. She looked around at the boy mess that was her world now. Greasy little hand marks smeared the walls, toy tanks, plastic guns, broken crayons, large sheets of scribbled on paper, and a package of magic markers, all scattered across the floor. *I know what I can do*, she thought and hurried over to the box of markers. She pulled out the red and brown markers, grabbed a tampon, and ducked into the upstairs bathroom. She took the tampon out of its wrapper, removed the applicator, and began scribbling all over it with the red and brown markers. She dropped the tampon into the toilet and watched the red and brown ink swirl together in the toilet water. It was a beautiful, slow color dance.

She sat on the toilet until she saw a blue eyeball peeking through the keyhole. Without flushing, she got up and walked out of the bathroom. Minutes later, she heard one of her cousins yelling, "Gross! What *is* that?" Less than ten minutes after that, there was a soft knock at the door.

"Chloe?"

"Yeah, come in."

Her aunt opened the door, slipped in the room and carefully shut the door behind her. "Unfortunately, we are surrounded by a bunch of guys, and half of them don't know what's going on, and I'm doing everything I can to put off explaining the facts of life to them, and god knows your uncle's not going to explain anything, so if you could be so kind as to make sure your used tampons aren't floating in the toilet, I would really appreciate it."

"I didn't flush?" she asked, feigning embarrassment.

"No, sweetheart." She smiled. Chloe thought the smile looked phony. "Just make sure everything's disposed of properly before you leave the bathroom." She turned toward the door and paused. She turned back to Chloe, as if she were going to ask a question, thought better of it, and then left the room.

Silas and Chloe

"Hey, Mom, is it okay if my science partner comes over to study this evening?" Silas asked as he held up the phone, receiver covered.

"Sure," she said from her seat in front of the TV. "Is it Eric?" she asked.

"No, the partners were assigned." He uncovered the receiver, "How about six o'clock? Cool. See you then."

At six o'clock, the doorbell rang. Silas buzzed Chloe up. When she walked in the front hall, Silas was suddenly very conscious of how she might perceive his home. He saw the smudges around the light switch and the ceiling cobwebs in the corner. There were times when he was ashamed of living in a two-bedroom condominium, and times when he felt guilty for feeling ashamed. "Come on in," Silas said, and made a grand bowing gesture. "Welcome to the palace," he said as he stepped aside, allowing her to walk past.

"Thanks," Chloe said. "Should I take off my shoes?"

"Oh, no, don't worry about it," Silas said.

Silas saw his mom sit up in her chair and crane her neck when she heard a female voice. "Let me show you around," Silas said as he shut the door behind Chloe. "This tour may take a few hours," he said, and smiled. "I'm just kidding," Silas felt the need to say. "Really, it's just your average two-bedroom condo."

"Funny," Chloe said, and smiled.

Silas led the way into the living room. "Mom, I'd like you to meet Chloe. She's my lab partner."

Silas's mom held her hand out, not bothering to get up. "Hello," she said. Chloe took her hand between both of hers and shook it. Silas's mom looked surprised. "So, you two are studying?" she asked.

"Yes, ma'am," Chloe said, releasing her hand.

"What exactly are you studying?" she asked.

"We have to pass a lab exam before Mr. Armand will let us in the lab for experiments."

"Well, have fun," she said. She picked up the remote and turned back to the TV. Silas and Chloe walked back to Silas's bedroom.

After about ten minutes of small talk about science and school, Silas and Chloe began studying. They read silently and then quizzed each other on what they had read, and then they read some more and quizzed each other again. Silas lay on the floor, his pillow wedged under his armpits, his hands propping up his head, and his textbook and worksheets spread out in front of him. Chloe had slipped off her shoes and was sitting cross-legged on Silas's bed. Her textbook was in her lap and worksheets were spread in a half circle around her. Just shy of an hour had passed when they heard a knocking on the door.

"Yeah," Silas called from the floor. His mom opened the door with one hand, balancing a faded fiberglass TV tray on her opposite forearm. Silas jumped up to help her.

"What's all this?" he asked, as he helped her maneuver the tray to his desk. His mom leaned back and waved her hand over the tray as if she were a game show host.

"Well, I brought you some sliced apples," she pointed, "and a couple glasses of orange juice. Chloe, I hope you like OJ," she paused. Chloe nodded. "And I also brought you some grapes. Oh, and some mints." She looked up at Silas.

"Thanks, Mom. You didn't have to…"

"No problem," she said and turned to go. "You two behave in here," she said, as she pulled the door closed.

"That was *so* nice of her," Chloe said.

"That was embarrassing," Silas said, blushing. "Oh?"

"Ahhh, yeah. She was really checking up on us."

"Huh?" Chloe asked. She looked confused.

"You know, to make sure we were *actually* studying… It's annoying," Silas said. He could feel his ears turning red.

"Aww, I think it's kinda sweet, you know, innocent," Chloe smiled. She stepped over the papers on the floor and grabbed an apple slice and a juice glass. She sat back down on the edge of the bed and sipped the juice. "You're lucky she cares," Chloe said. "My mom doesn't give a shit about me, let alone about some guy in my room." Silas looked up at Chloe. There was a moment where they made eye contact, and he thought they connected.

Silence...

"Say..." Chloe said, breaking the silence that had gone from potentially interesting to painfully awkward, "do you mind if I use your bathroom? I always like to brush my teeth after I eat."

"Sure," Silas said. He got up and showed her to the bathroom. She carried her backpack with her.

"Thanks," she said as she closed the bathroom door.

"I'll be in my room," Silas called through the door.

"Okay," Chloe said.

She came back to the room a few minutes later. "I should probably get going," she said, packing up her papers and books.

"Sure, I'll drive you home," Silas said.

"You don't have to," she said as she made her way to the bedroom door.

"I insist," Silas said as he grabbed his keys from the desk. "It's getting dark."

"Thanks," she said.

The five-minute ride to her house was silent.

"Well, thanks for coming over," Silas said.

"Thanks for having me. Oh, and please thank your mom for me for the snack," Chloe said as she got out. "I'll see you tomorrow."

"See you tomorrow." Silas smiled and waved at her. She returned the smile and shut the car door. Silas watched as she walked up the sidewalk. When she got to the door, she turned, waved, and disappeared inside.

Silas

Silas went to brush his teeth before bed and noticed that Chloe had left her toothbrush. It was balanced on the edge of the porcelain sink, the bristles hanging hygienically in the air over the edge. The area around it looked very neat, as if a certain amount of attention had been paid to the cleaning up of the area. For reasons he couldn't quite explain, this surprised him.

When he picked up her toothbrush, he felt excitement. Holding her toothbrush felt very intimate; he held it up to the light and examined it, like it might offer some insight into her soul. He saw the water trapped between the white and blue bristles. He looked intently and thought about the water that had been in her mouth and the bristles that had passed through her lips and brushed over her tongue. Compared to his toothbrush, her toothbrush was immaculate. His toothbrush had toothpaste caked around his handle, and hers was almost perfect, except some of the bristles were curled back down onto themselves. He brought her toothbrush to his lips and wanted to kiss it, and then he considered brushing his teeth with it. He caught a glimpse of himself in the mirror on the other side of the toothbrush. *Quit being such a fucking weirdo,* he thought.

When he finished brushing his teeth, with his toothbrush, he took hers to the kitchen, pulled a Ziploc baggie from the drawer, and dropped it into the bag. He set the plastic bag on top of his backpack so he wouldn't forget to give it to Chloe in school the next day.

Chloe

The sound of children whining and screaming greeted Chloe as she stepped inside the house. *I so don't wanna be here,* she thought. It was dusk and the room lights hadn't been turned on yet, which gave the house a haunted feeling as the long shadows crawled up the walls. Chloe quietly floated from one room to the other, drifting to the back of the house. If her aunt knew she was home, she'd put her to work, wanting her to help get the kids ready for bed. She stood in the middle of the dusk-tinged kitchen and listened to her cousins' shattering squeals. She tiptoed down the hall and silently stepped out the back door.

She inhaled the cool evening air and started walking…anywhere. As she walked, thoughts of Silas kept exploding in her head. *What was that awkward moment all about, anyway? Did I read that all wrong, or did he want to kiss me? There's no way he wanted to kiss me. He could do so much better. He's too nice. And, I'm pregnant. No decent high school guy wants to date a pregnant girl, especially if it's someone else's baby.*

She stopped at the train tracks and looked up at the fingernail sliver of a moon dangling in the darkening sky. The dull light from the setting sun made her feel like she was a ghost, like she wasn't actually living this moment, like it wasn't her life.

Maybe he's so nice that it wouldn't matter, She let herself think. *Maybe he'd love me so deeply, and care about me so much that he'd want to raise the baby as his own?* She looked down at the tracks. She heard the faint sound of the train horn blowing in the distance. It reminded her of the baby screams that troubled her dreams. She watched the engine's white light, a dot in the distance, as it slowly approached; its whistle regularly announcing its impending arrival. *Who am I kidding?* She stepped in between the tracks and stared at the light coming toward her. She heard the rumble of the train as it got closer. *My life sucks.*

The ground shook with the approaching train. All noise was train noise. It was just the train and her thoughts. *Is this worth it? Is life worth it?* The deafening blast of the train horn scared her. She thought of her baby. She leaped off of the tracks just as the train roared past. The whoosh of the passing engine blew her skirt against her legs. *Silas,* she thought, *just maybe...* A strange confluence of hope and despair welled up behind her eyes. She wiped away the tears with the back of her hand and walked to her aunt's house.

Silas and Chloe

When Silas got to school, he went to his locker and then went to find Chloe. "Hey, Chloe," he said.

"Oh, hi, Silas," she said as she paused from searching her locker and smiled at him.

"You left this at my place last night," he said, and held the clear plastic bag by the edge; it unrolled to reveal her toothbrush. She snatched it from him and buried it in her pocket. She blushed and looked around to see if anyone had noticed. Two girls had noticed and laughed. As they walked away, they giggled and leaned into each other, whispering the whole way up the hallway.

"Oh great," Chloe said as she pulled out a book and slammed her locker shut.

"What?" Silas asked.

"That's all I need," Chloe said.

"What? What'd I do?"

"It hasn't been easy to meet people here. Everyone's been in their little cliques since *forever*, and now you come along and give me my toothbrush

71

in front of the whole world, like I spent the night at your house or something." Chloe marched to her class.

"Listen," Silas said, trying to keep up and carry on a conversation, "Would it really be so bad if people thought we were dating?"

Chloe stopped and turned to Silas, "No, that wouldn't be that bad, but they're going to call me a slut for sleeping with you. That's what's bad!"

"But you didn't sleep with me."

"I know that, and you know that, but believe me, by lunch everybody else will think we fucked."

"I don't think so," Silas said, wanting to reassure her, wanting to calm her down.

"I've been through this before." Tears began to well. "At my last school, people called me a slut." She wiped her eyes and walked into class. Silas stood there looking in the classroom, not knowing what to do or say. He was sorry he even brought the stupid fucking toothbrush to school in the first place.

Chloe

"This is complete bullshit," she muttered as she peeked into the dimly lit shower room. "Fucking community showers," she hissed and walked back to her gym locker. At her other school, the physical education class consisted of walking around the gym, wearing a pedometer, logging your steps, and talking to your friends as you went. There was no shower at the end. And now, at this school, she had to take a shower after each PE class, or she'd get in trouble.

Fortunately, there was a way around the mandatory shower. She noticed that all of the other girls kept their underwear on, pushed their bra straps off of their shoulders, wrapped a towel around themselves, and walked past the PE teacher's office window. The PE teacher would sit in her yellow office, the florescent light buzzing, and check the girls' names off of her clipboard as they walked to the shower. They'd get there, turn on the nozzle, barely getting their hair wet, and walk past the teacher again, this time with wet hair. Problem solved.

In the shower, when she leaned forward to dampen her long hair, her towel slipped. She caught it just before it hit the wet floor. While she was pulling her hair back to rewrap her towel, she heard someone talking to her.

"You're that new girl from Wisconsin, aren't you?"

"I'm actually from Illinois, downstate." Chloe said, now scrambling to wrap her towel back around herself.

"Oh, my god, you've got a little pooch there, don't you?" another girl said and pointed to her belly.

"Do you drink a lot of beer in Wisconsin?" another girl asked, "Because that sure looks like a beer gut to me."

"It looks like she's pregnant to me," the first girl said. The two girls laughed.

"Is that it? Are you a *bad girl* who's gone and got herself knocked up?"

"You're the slut who slept with her science partner, Silas, aren't you?"

Chloe hurried back to her locker and frantically got dressed. She saw the two girls come out of the shower, laughing. They slinked past her.

"Slut," one of them hissed.

"Whore," the other one snipped.

Chloe ran out of the locker room without waiting to be dismissed. She hurried to the nearest bathroom. She tried to maintain her composure, not wanting to lose her shit in the hallway. She ducked into the nearest bathroom and locked the stall door and sat down on the black toilet seat; she leaned back, raised her feet, and slammed them into the stall door. The harsh sound reverberated angrily off of the bathroom's brick walls. "FUCK YOU!" she yelled to an empty bathroom.

Silas and Chloe

Silas's bedroom windows were black with night. The lamp on his desk cast a warm yellow circle of light, leaving the edges of the room dark. "Don't cry," Silas said as he handed Chloe a box of Kleenex. She took it without looking up.

"I'm so sorry, Chloe. I didn't mean for things to get bad for you. I'm so stupid. Fucking toothbrush," Silas said.

Chloe looked up from the tissue. "Oh no, don't blame yourself," she said and dried her eyes. "Rumors were spreading even before the toothbrush." She looked into Silas's eyes. "I'm sorry you're involved now. I didn't mean to drag you into this world of shit."

"What are you talking about, dragging me into this?" Silas asked.

"Well, some girls started a rumor that I was pregnant, and that I was a slut who would blow anyone for five dollars." Chloe paused to put the tissue box back on the desk. She continued, embarrassed, not looking at Silas. "Then boys started waving five-dollar bills at me when I'd walked down the hall." Silas looked down at the carpet. "You don't believe what they say about me, do you?" Chloe asked.

"No. No, I don't," he said.

"So, when you brought the bag with my toothbrush in it, you know?" she said, expecting him to catch on and understand without having to say anymore.

"Know what?" Silas asked.

"Well, now the people are saying that the baby is yours." She stopped and watched Silas's face for a reaction. "I'm sorry," she whispered. Her head fell into her open hands.

"You know what?" Silas asked.

Chloe shook her head, "No, what?"

"Fuck them," he said. "There's a party this Friday in Chicago. This kid's dad is a landlord and he has an empty apartment, so the kid's throwing a party there before his dad rents the place out. I think you and I should go together and show the haters that we don't give a shit what they say. Fuck them."

"It doesn't bother you that they say I'm a whore who charges five dollars for a blow job?"

"You can pay for the gas, then." He smiled. She grabbed a pillow from his bed and started hitting him with it. He grabbed her by her waist and pulled her to him. Before either really knew what was happening, she was lying on top of him on the floor, his hands around her waist, the pillow wedged between them. They stared at each other. Silas kissed Chloe.

Just then, there was a knock at the door. "Silas," his mother's voice interrupted. They scrambled up into sitting positions just as the door opened. His mother paused and said, "It's almost eleven. I think you should probably drive Chloe home now." She turned and walked out, leaving the door open behind her.

Chloe

Chloe fumbled with the house key in the dark as Silas watched from his car. The greenish glow of the car's dash lit his face. *He's so patient, he'll make a good father,* she thought. The key clanged against the lock. Chloe thought the dark made everything seem louder. She was uneasy; she had never come back to her aunt's place this late. Her aunt hadn't really laid out any ground rules for her, though. Still, she was nervous.

She finally unlocked the door and waved to Silas before she ducked inside. He waved back and drove away. She went to her room and quietly felt her way through the night-light-lit bedroom. She tried not to wake the boys. She laid down on her lumpy floor mattress and pulled the thin blanket to her chin and thought about Silas. She felt a surge of what seemed like electricity course through her veins when she thought about him. He didn't know she was pregnant, but for some reason she didn't worry about it.

She thought about how Silas's mom cared enough to check in on them. Chloe liked that. She wanted that. She wondered if Silas was finally the person who would care for her. She imagined sharing Silas's bed. She imagined sleeping on clean sheets and waking up under his heavy comforter. She imagined walking out to the kitchen where Silas's mom would have pulp-free orange juice and Coco Puffs ready for her at the table. The kitchen would smell like toast and coffee.

Silas

"Mom," Silas called as he twisted into his shoes in the front hallway.

"Yeah," she answered from the living room.

"I'm heading out."

"Come here a minute," she said. He appeared before her in the living room. "Where are you going?"

"I'm going to a party," he said.

"Where's this party?"

"In the city."

"Why do you have to go all the way to Chicago to go to a party? Why can't you go to a party here, in town?"

"Mom, everyone's going."

"Everyone?" she asked and raised her eyebrows.

"Come on, you know what I mean. All of my friends."

"Is Eric going?"

"I don't know. Maybe."

"What do you mean, maybe?" she asked.

"Eric and I don't really hang out much anymore," he said and shrugged.

"Why? He's been your best friend since first grade."

"Come on, Mom. I don't really have time for stupid questions."

"Well who's going to be there then?"

"Seriously? More stupid questions?"

"I'm your mom. I have a right to ask you *stupid* questions."

"Last time I went to a party, you didn't seem to care. You told me to have fun and not to get a venereal disease, remember?"

"Speaking of venereal diseases, is that girl you've been studying with going?"

"Chloe?"

"Is that her name? Chloe?"

"Yes."

"Yes what? Yes, that's her name, or yes she's going?"

"Yes to both. That's her name, and I'm picking her up."

"Silas, I've got a bad feeling about that girl," his mom said. "I know her type. She was raised rough. She's had a hard life. A girl like that can't give. She doesn't know how to give. She only knows how to take, how to survive because that's all she's been able to do. She's a taker, not a giver. You deserve better. You deserve a giver."

"Quit being so dramatic, Mom," Silas said. "She's a nice girl. She hasn't asked me for anything. You don't even *know* her. I mean, you've seen her like twice now. You can't sit there and tell me that you know her type."

"Listen, honey, I'm only telling you this because I care for you. You're at an age where your mistakes start to count for the rest of your life."

"Mom, there's nothing wrong with her," he said, and pulled his phone from his pocket to check the time.

"Am I keeping you from something?"

"Mom, really? Can I just go?"

"Silas, she's bad news. I wish you'd find a nice girl." She got up and headed to the kitchen. Silas followed, wanting his mom to say her piece and then let him go to the party.

"Mom, she's a good person."

"She's bad news," his mom said, and turned around and looked him in the eye. "Call it women's intuition."

"Ha!" Silas chortled. "Women's intuition?"

"Yes."

"A lot of good that's done you," Silas said.

"What's that supposed to mean?"

"I mean your track record with guys sucks. How many guys have you thought were *the one* since Dad? How many?"

As soon as the words left Silas's mouth his mom's open palm slammed into the side of his face. It brought tears to his eyes, and he could taste blood.

"Get out of here," she said through clenched teeth. She stomped to her room and slammed the door. As he left, Silas was sure to slam the door, too.

Silas and Chloe

Silas took the back route from the suburbs to Chicago to avoid any remnant rush-hour traffic on the interstate. The cookie-cutter houses gradually gave way to brick buildings that seemed to grow toward the sky with each passing mile. "I'd love to go for a walk down here because…" Chloe said as they neared Chicago. Silas waited for her to finish her thought, but nothing more came.

"Okay, I'll bite," he said. "Why would you love to go for a walk down here?"

"Because you can see into peoples' lit-up windows in the evening, you know? You get to peek into their lives, you know?"

"You're a Peeping Tom," Silas said.

"I'm not a Peeping Tom. I just like to see what people've done with their apartments, you know. I like to see how others live their lives. That doesn't make me a Peeping Tom." Chloe settled back in her seat and seemed upset.

Silence…

"Don't you love how the city lights twinkle in the night?" Chloe said.

"I love Chicago," Silas said.

"I've never been here before," Chloe said. "I've never seen Chicago." She looked to Silas as he was driving. "The biggest city I've ever seen was Decatur."

"We'll have to get you down here to do the tourist thing," Silas said as he checked the directions on his phone. He turned off of Peterson onto Lincoln Avenue.

"Oh, my god," Chloe said in awe. "Look at these dumpy little motels." She smiled and leaned forward in her seat to get a better look.

"I've always thought that this stretch would make a great set for a movie about hookers and junkies," Silas said.

"If I could be a fly on the wall in one of those motel rooms," Chloe said. "Do you realize how many stories happen in places like that? Every day?" She put her hands on the passenger-door ledge and stared. "I bet they even rent those rooms by the hour," she said. "I bet they'd rent them to minors, too." She looked back to Silas, "If I ever run away, this is where I'll be. Remember that, Silas, if I ever disappear, check for me here first." She sat back in her seat, put her hands in her lap, and continued to look out the window.

At a stoplight, Silas studied her reflection in the passenger window. He reached for her hand; she grabbed his. The yellow glow from the streetlights washed over them: dark, then light, then dark, then light. He loved feeling the weight of her hand.

Silas parked the car and they walked to the apartment. Silas opened the trunk and pulled out a camouflage sleeping bag; he slung it over his shoulder. Chloe looked at the sleeping bag and then at Silas.

"What?" Silas asked.

"Is that really necessary?"

"There's probably not any furniture in there. It's an empty apartment," Silas said.

There was an old couple watching from the deck above. Silas waved; they ignored him and mumbled something to each other. Silas and Chloe walked down the steps, through the backdoor, and into the kitchen. Silas walked over to the refrigerator and pulled out two beers, handed one to Chloe, and popped his can opened his with casual nonchalance. The kitchen opened up into a dining room area. Toward the front was a living area.

In the dining room there was a paint-speckled radio next to a stack of painting tarps that the painters had left. Classic rock was playing through buzzing speakers that crackled with each bass note that passed through them. Everybody was sitting on the floor, drinking beer and playing a card game. From what Silas could tell, they were playing a drinking version of strip poker. Everyone was at various stages of being undressed, and they would collectively drink at certain points in the game. Someone would yell, "Drink," and they would all take large swigs of their chosen alcohol. Silas and Chloe stood there in the crowded room and watched.

"Hey!" a shirtless guy slurred from the floor. "You two wanna play?"

"Eh, I don't think so," Silas said. He politely nodded at the guy. "Thanks, though."

"She won't play because she doesn't want anyone to see her baby bump," a girl called from the side of the room. Silas's head snapped toward the voice. It was Bree. She was sitting cross-legged on the floor, wearing only a white bra, shorts, and socks. Silas stared at her tan breasts spilling over the too-small bra. "You like what you see?" Bree asked Silas. She laughed and held her hands out to her sides, drawing attention to her breasts. "You could'a had this," she said, shaking her shoulders back and forth, her chest jiggling, "but you're too much of a pussy. You just sat there, doing nothing. I'm glad nothing happened, though. It looks like you don't use protection. Got your girlfriend all knocked up and everything." She pointed to Chloe with the neck of her beer bottle.

Silas could tell she was drunk. Chloe squeezed Silas's hand.

"She's such a bitch," Chloe whispered, loud enough for everyone to hear.

"Some pretty bold words from a slut," Bree said.

"Let's go," Silas said and turned to walk away. Chloe's hand slipped from his. He turned just in time to see Chloe hurl her full can of beer at Bree's head. Bree blocked it; there was a loud thunk as the full beer can hit Bree's forearms, spraying everywhere. Bree sprang to her feet and charged at Chloe.

"Fucking bitch," Bree screamed. Silas stepped between them. Bree began pounding on his chest with both hands. "Get out of the way, you fucking homo," she yelled, her tiny fists opening to claws and scratching Silas's face. Everyone else backed to the edges of the room.

"Police, police, police," someone yelled from the other room. People sprinted for the back door. They climbed over each other to get out. Bree stopped her barrage and ran back to collect her shoes and shirt. She ran for the back door along with everyone else.

Silas and Chloe were swept out the door with the rest of the partygoers. Silas looked up and saw the old couple on the deck; they were sitting there, smiling, drinking beer, and enjoying the chaos that they most likely had instigated. Silas and Chloe were hyper-vigilant as they walked back to the car.

Silas started the car and drove down the one-way avenue bathed in yellow city streetlights. He pulled up to the stop sign and waited for partygoers to cross. He saw Bree's friends crossing, and then he saw Bree fumbling along behind them, trying to keep up while putting on her shoes. His leg tensed when Bree stepped in front of his car. He pushed on the brake pedal as hard as he could. He felt his shoe sliding off the edge. The harder he pushed, the more it slid.

There was a ghastly snapping sound as his foot slid off of the break and landed square on the accelerator. The car lurched forward and hit Bree mid-thigh; her legs were cut out from under her. She landed on the hood of his car with a dull thud. The sound reverberated throughout the frame of the car.

Silas saw a horrified look on Bree's face as she lay sprawled across the hood of the car. The momentum of the impact carried her long brown hair all the way to the windshield where it fanned out against the glass. Silas instinctively reached out to touch it, but pulled back when he touched glass. He shook his head, trying not to see it all, trying to shake it all off.

He reflexively threw the car in reverse and slammed the accelerator to the floor. His tires screeched. Bree slid off the hood. Her body thumped to the pavement. Her friends screamed as they ran to her. Silas stopped the car halfway down the block and watched as Bree's friends all gathered around her. They went for their cell phones, dialed, looked at Bree, and then stared down Silas. He reversed the car all the way down the block, backed around the corner, and drove away.

"Holy fuck," Chloe said. "Did that just happen?" Silas's knuckles were pink and white as he strangled the steering wheel. "Silas, are you okay?" Chloe asked. He sat there, quiet. "Silas, pull over," she said. Silas pulled over and stared ahead into the night.

"What just happened?" he asked.

"Silas, you need to get your shit together. Right now!" Chloe said.

"Honestly, what just happened?"

"Silas, get out of the car. I'm driving," Chloe said. Silas obeyed. He walked over toward Chloe's side, but stopped when he got to the front of the car. He stared at the hood.

"What did I do?" he asked and touched the hood of the car. The streetlight's reflection on the hood was disrupted by the fresh dents. Silas saw a splat of blood and clump of hair wedged in the seam of the car. He began to cry. Chloe took him by the hand and guided him to the passenger seat. He sat. She shut the door and ran around to the driver's side.

"We're going to need some cash," she said as she buckled her seatbelt.

"Do you think she's alright?" Silas asked.

"She'll be fine. Her friends were calling for help as we were leaving." She stopped and studied

Silas. "We need to get out of here. Give me your ATM card." Silas reached into his back pocket, pulled out his wallet, and handed her the whole thing. She drove to the Jewel parking lot.

"What are we doing here?"

"We're going in," Chloe said.

"I'll stay here," he said.

"You can't. Get what you want from the car. We're leaving it here," she said and slammed the door. Silas sat there. Chloe walked around and pounded on his window. "Get the fuck out of the car, Silas," she screamed. Startled, he dragged himself out of the car. Chloe grabbed his hand and dragged him across the parking lot. Silas followed, heavy-footed. She was going so fast that she had to stop and wait for the automated doors of the grocery store to open so she didn't run into them. She marched Silas over to the ATM. She pulled the cash card from his wallet and slid it into the machine.

"Okay, what's your number?"

Silas just stood there. "Huh?"

"Your PIN? What's your PIN number?"

"Oh, three, three, three, three."

"Four threes?" Chloe asked. Silas nodded his head. She frantically punched in the numbers in and hit more buttons as the machine beeped its responses. "How come it won't let me take out five-hundred dollars?"

"There's a daily limit. I think it's 250 dollars."

Chloe hit more buttons, and the machine spit out cash. She grabbed it and looked around as if she just realized that there might be others nearby, as if she just realized they weren't alone. She saw the cameras in the ceiling. Her eyes got big with worry.

"What is it, Chloe?" Silas asked.

"Nothing. We've gotta go," she said, and walked out of the brightly lit store. She was no longer holding Silas's hand. He had to run to catch up to her.

"Chloe, the car's over there," he said, and pointed across the parking lot strewn with puddles and litter.

"We're done with the car. Leave it."

"But that's my car. We can't just leave it there."

"Trust me, it'll be all right. Just leave it there for now."

"Where are we going?" he asked.

"We're going to the motels."

Chloe

"How'd you get us this room?" Silas asked as he looked around. The ceiling was bubbled and water-stained in the corner by the door.

"I paid a guy twenty bucks to rent it for us," Chloe said. She kicked off her shoes and plopped down on the bed, her back resting against the headboard. She reached over, grabbed the remote control and started flipping through the channels. "Hey! We get HBO," she said, "for free." Silas sat on the edge of the bed and stared at the wood paneling across from him. His shoulders wilted.

"Come up here by me," Chloe said and patted the bed. Silas scooted back across the bed next to her. He laid his head on her shoulder, wrapped his arms around her waist and shut his eyes. She smiled and ran her fingers through his hair. He fell asleep, and she turned her attention to the movie *Say Anything* on HBO. She loved it when Lloyd Dobler stood outside of Diane Court's house and played the song "In Your Eyes" on a boom box held high above his head. She thought that was so romantic.

Chloe caught a glimpse of herself in the mirror across the room and smiled at the reflection of Silas asleep on her shoulder. "This is romantic, too," she whispered, "in its own way."

Silas

Silas woke up confused. Everything was unrecognizable. He tried to focus. *Why's the TV on? I don't recognize this blanket. That's not my bedroom window...* And then the heavy events fell onto his mind like a punch to the nose. His heart sank when he realized it wasn't a dream, and it wasn't going to disappear simply because he was awake.

It was still dark out. The red digits said it was 3:03 a.m. His mind raced. His heart raced. He got up and walked around and around and around the room. He looked at Chloe. *How can she sleep right now?* He wanted to wake her up. He wanted to talk about her plan. *She had a plan, right? She knew what she was doing, right?*

He sat in the wicker-backed chair at the table in the corner of the room. He lifted the blinds and peeked out the window. He marveled at how bright the city at night was compared to the suburbs. *Light at night just distorts the truth. Light creates shadows,* he thought. He stared at Chloe and was suddenly overcome with gratitude. *I was the one who hit Bree, not her, and she stayed with me. She took control of a shitty situation, got us this room and everything. She didn't have to do that.* He was suddenly okay with her sleeping. *She deserves to get some rest.*

Silas and Chloe

Silas crawled back into bed with Chloe at about 5:30 in the morning. He put his arm around her waist and pulled her to him. She groggily woke up, turned over, and looked at him; she smiled. He propped himself up on his elbow and tucked an errant strand of hair behind her ear. He leaned in and kissed her. She wound her arms around his neck and returned his kiss. His hands slowly made their way under her shirt and slid up the curves of her smooth side. Silas worked his way around to the back of her bra. She laughed through their mashed lips.

"What? What's so funny?" he asked, play-biting her lip.

"My bra... It fastens in the front," she whispered in his ear. He reached around to the front. He suddenly stopped. His arm recoiled. He stared at her.

"What is it?" she asked, staring at him.

"What's *that*?" He asked, shocked.

"What's what?"

"Are you pregnant?" he asked, sitting up beside her.

Chloe sat up straight and gathered the brown comforter tight up under her arms, hiding her belly. She sat there and stared at Silas, waiting for his words to fall out of his gaping mouth.

Silence...

"I don't mean to be rude, but when I went for your bra, your belly felt like it was... Like it was pregnant," Silas said.

"Silas, I love you," Chloe said, pulling him to her.

"I-I love you, too, I guess," he said, resisting.

"You guess?"

"Well, it's kinda hard for me to figure things out if I feel like I'm not getting the full picture."

"It was a mistake. He was terrible to me. He used to hit me," she begged.

"Who? The father?" Silas asked.

"He's back home, downstate," she said. "My mom didn't want me seeing him after he hit me. I guess someone from the school called DCFS because of my absences and the bruises, and all of that was interfering with my mom's *new life* with her *new boyfriend.* She's so selfish."

Silas sat there, staring at his foot.

"Please say something," Chloe said.

"I'm not sure what to say."

"Silas, I'm so in love with you. I never knew life could be so good. I know I can be someone different with you, someone better."

"Someone different?" Silas asked.

"I don't have to be like my mom. I don't have to end up like her," Chloe said. "Silas, please don't let this ruin a good thing. I'm not the same person I was before I met you. I've changed, and I owe it all to you." She reached for his hand. He let her hold it. She pulled him to her with both hands. "I love you, Silas," she said, and kissed his lips.

"Hey?" he said, gently pushing her away.

"Yeah?" she asked, her eyes still closed.

"What are we going to do?" he asked.

"About what?"

"About getting home?" Silas asked.

"I'm working on it," she said, and kissed him again.

"Okay," he mumbled, and slid under the comforter with her. He chuckled as she wrapped her arms around him.

"What's so funny?" she asked, pulling back a little.

"My mom named me Silas because it means third, like I was the third person in the family, and now, here I am, the third person in our little family."

Chloe smiled, and wrapped herself completely around Silas.

Chloe

Chloe's stomach screamed for food. She swung her feet out from under the brown comforter and put on her clothes and shoes. She peeked out the window at the quiet morning; the only sounds were the low ramblings of the TV and a hypnotic white noise that came from the passing cars on Lincoln Avenue. She watched Silas as he slept and then looked to see what time it was. The numbers burned a digital red: 10:07 a.m. Her stomach rumbled. She feared the sound would wake Silas, but it didn't. His deep rhythmic breathing continued, uninterrupted.

She tiptoed across the worn carpet to where Silas's jeans were draped over a wicker-backed chair. She rummaged through his pockets until she found his phone and his motel key and slipped them both into her pocket. She walked over to the motel phone on the bedside stand and followed its cord from the base of the phone to the wall socket behind the stand. She unplugged it from the wall, put the plastic end in her mouth, and bit down hard on the square adapter. She felt the piece crack between her molars, and little plastic shards populated her mouth. She spray-spit the miniscule plastic pieces onto the carpet behind the bed and halfheartedly reinserted the shattered square into the plug, knowing that it would no longer work. She didn't want him to call anyone without checking with her. She grabbed a piece of paper and wrote:

> *Dear Silas,*
> *It's 10:15 and I'm super hungry. I went to the*
> *store to get us some food. I'll be back soon.*
>
> *I LOVE YOU!*
>
> *Love,*
> *Chloe*

She propped the note up against the mustard-colored phone so that if he woke, looking for her, that'd be the first thing he'd see. She quietly pulled the door shut behind her and turned to the open parking lot. She took in a deep breath of late morning air. She thought she could smell Lake Michigan and feel its humidity in her lungs and at that moment she realized how stuffy the motel room had become.

Silas

A Honda Civic came roaring at Silas and hit him mid-thigh. He didn't feel the pain, but knew it was there. He felt the thin metal of the car hood crumple under his face as he landed on it. As he fell in slow motion, he saw his own face in the driver's seat. He studied it. He saw fear. He saw sadness. And he saw anger. He was ashamed of the anger. He began crying.

And that's how he woke up. Crying. He rolled over in the bed and saw the note that Chloe had left. He got up, went to the sink, and splashed cold water on his face. He searched the mirror for the anger he had seen in his dream, but couldn't see past the worry that had carved new lines in his face. He went to the chair and pulled on his jeans. He could tell from the weight of his jeans that something was missing. He pulled them on and patted his pockets; he realized his phone was gone. *Maybe Chloe took it,* he thought as he got on his hands and knees and looked under the table.

He felt lonely. He wanted to talk to someone about everything… about anything. He wanted to get out of the motel room. He wanted to go home. The bubble he had inhabited with Chloe a few hours before had burst with the reality of what had happened. She wasn't there; he could no longer hide from what he'd done. He was alone with it, alone with the fresh memories.

He sat down, the strained wicker backing groaned at the sudden weight. *What now?* He wanted to call his mom. He knew she'd help him out. *She'd know what to do.*

He walked over to the mustard-yellow phone, sat down on the bed, picked up the receiver, and dialed home. He put the receiver to his ear and heard nothing. He waited, but still-nothing. He hung up and tried again. Nothing. "Fuck," he said as he slammed the phone down in its cradle. He leaned back against the bed's headrest. He noticed that there was no give; it was bolted to the wall. He looked around the room at the generic prints of Midwestern landscapes; their faux wood frames were all screwed to the wall. Silas felt like a criminal. He wasn't going to steal the fucking paintings off of the wall. He felt like the room was passing judgment on him. He opened the curtains. When he saw outside, he realized that he had to go home, that he had to face the consequences. If he could only talk to his mom, she'd know what to do. She'd help him.

Silas and Chloe

Silas heard what seemed like someone gently kicking the motel room door. "Chloe? Is that you?" he asked.

"Yeah. Open the door. My hands are full." Silas got up and opened the door. She stood there with her hands full of light brown plastic bags from Jewel.

"You went to Jewel?"

"Yup," she said.

"Did you see my car? Is it still there?"

"Yeah, it's still there," she said. "I got us some good stuff." Silas reached down and helped her with the bags. They set them on the table and she began pulling items out, as if it were show and tell. "I got us some Cocoa Puffs," she said as she pulled the box from the bag. "And some skim milk." She pulled out a half gallon of milk. "And, I even remembered to get some plastic spoons," she said, proud of herself.

"We don't have a refrigerator. What are we gonna to do with the milk?"

"We'll just have to eat the Cocoa Puffs first," she said. "I got us some new toothbrushes, too." She waved the packages in the air. "A blue one for you and a pink one for me." She put them on the table and dipped her hand into the bag again. "I also got you this and this," she said, as pulled a plastic liter of vodka and a box of generic sleeping pills from a plastic bag.

"Why?" Silas asked.

"To help you sleep," she said. "My mom swore by vodka and sleeping pills. It'll help. Trust me."

"How'd you get that?" Silas asked as he pointed to the bottle of vodka. "I mean, you're not old enough to buy alcohol."

"That Jewel has a self-checkout. I just pretended like I swiped it, and bagged it, real quick like, no problem. No one noticed. It's heaven for shoplifters." She smiled as she unpacked the rest of the food. "Potato chips, soda, all the good stuff," she said. "You know, I really liked shopping for us." She wadded up all of the plastic bags and crammed them into the small garbage can under the bathroom sink.

"Do you know what happened to my phone?" Silas asked.

Chloe stood up, and without looking at him said, "I threw it out."

"You threw it out? My iPhone! Do have any idea how much that cost me?" Silas yelled.

"No I don't, but really, do we want the police tracking it back here to us?"

"I guess not, but you can't just make those decisions. We have to make them together. I really wanted to call my mom, and now I can't. The goddamn motel phone doesn't work," he said and gestured toward the phone.

"Why were you gonna to call your mom?" Chloe asked. She plopped down on the bed. "You know, you probably shouldn't. They've probably got her phone tapped." She fiddled with the hem of her skirt.

"You think so?" he asked.

"For sure," Chloe said.

"I just wanted to talk to her," Silas said. "I wanted to ask her what I need to do to get home."

"We're doing fine," Chloe said. "We're just fine right here. You don't need to call your mom." She examined her thumbnail, "Besides, I don't think your mom likes me."

"Chloe, we can't live like this. In a shitty motel room," he said, and knocked a plastic motel cup off of the counter. Chloe wiped tears from her eyes. "What? Why are you crying?" Silas asked. "It's me who's in trouble. It's me who hit Bree with my car, and it's me who took off like an asshole. Everyone knows it was me," Silas said, his voice had wound itself up an octave.

"Silas, what's going to happen to *me*?" Chloe cried. "You need to think about *me*, and *us*," she said and rubbed her belly.

"What do you mean? Nothing, probably," Silas said, confused.

"There's probably already a plan in place for you when you return. Your mom's probably already talked to the police. Hell, maybe she's even lawyered up already. It'll all be taken care of for you. But not for me." Chloe picked at the comforter. "Let's say my aunt and uncle know that I was involved in the hit and run." Silas flinched. "That's what it's called Silas, a hit and run. Anyway, what's going to happen to me? What's going to happen to the baby? My aunt sure as hell isn't going to let me stay there. And, what if I'm an accessory to the crime? Who's going to keep me out of juvie? No one, that's who." She looked at him, "*Please.* You're the only one who can help me. You're the only one who can protect me and take care of me."

Silas sat down. Chloe continued, "Even if things worked out for you *and* for me, think about the first day back at school. A lot of fun that'll be. And what if Bree's dead, or she has permanent brain damage, or some shit like that? What then? Things aren't going to be that smooth, are they?

"I just wanted call my mom to find out what's up, you know. This not knowing is driving me crazy. I can't sleep. I can't do anything. I just sit here and watch movies on HBO, and when I do sleep, I have bad dreams. We can't stay here forever. What happens when the money runs out?"

"We get more. You said your limit was 250 dollars a day, right?"

"Yeah, but the cash in there is left over from buying the car. That'll go fast. And, what if they close the account, or if they trace the withdrawals to the Jewel ATM, and they see us on surveillance cameras taking out cash or something?"

"Silas, we can make a life like this. I've run away before. Trust me, we can do this."

"But you're pregnant. What kind of life is that for your baby?" he asked.

"Please, please, promise me that you won't call your mom."

"Chloe, I'm going to have to call her sometime," Silas said. "Tomorrow. I'll go look for somewhere to make the call tomorrow."

"I can make the call for you tomorrow," Chloe said. "You can just stay here and relax. What if there are wanted posters with your name and picture on them, or if your face has been broadcast on the news or something, and then the police hunt you down? You wouldn't want that would you?"

"Chloe, I think this needs to end, so if that's how it ends, then that's how it ends," Silas said. "Tomorrow, I'm calling. You'll see, things will be all right. It'll all work out. Trust me. Mom will help us get out of this."

"I will not lose you, Silas," Chloe said, tears welling up in her eyes.

"Who said anything about you loosing me?" he asked. He sat down beside her and wiped the tears off of her cheek.

"If you call, that'll be the end of us, and I won't let it happen. You're the best thing that's ever happened to me. I won't let you go."

"You need to relax. Things'll work out for us."

"No they won't. What do you know? You've had things handed to you on a silver platter. You know nothing about real life." Chloe began sobbing, her face in her hands. Silas got up, walked over to her, and wrapped his arms around her.

Chloe smiled, got up, grabbed the plastic cup from off of the floor and took it over to the table where she mixed vodka with Sprite and handed the drink to Silas. "This'll calm you down." He took it from her and smelled it.

"You know what?" Silas asked.

"What?"

"I've only really been drunk once," he said.

"Bullshit," she said and raised her eyebrows.

"No, seriously. I've always carried the same full beer around at parties. No one ever noticed. Everyone's so into themselves and worried about how they look. I've never had more than a sip of alcohol in my life."

"It's no big deal," Chloe said. "It'll help you relax. Honestly."

Silas sipped it and then sucked air in between his teeth. "That's strong," he said. Chloe grabbed the Sprite and added more to the drink.

They cozied up to each other and watched TV. Over the course of the movie, Chloe served Silas stiff drinks. He downed them one after another. After serving Silas seven stiff drinks, Chloe gave him a hand full of sleeping pills. "Trust me, these will help you sleep," she said. "I know you haven't been sleeping well."

Silas reached out and took the pills from her. "It seems like a lot of pills," he said, sifting them around in his hand.

"Don't worry about it," Chloe said. "It'll be okay." Silas looked at her, his eyebrows raised. "Look, these aren't prescription. They're sold over the counter. They can't be dangerous if they're sold over the counter, right? Besides, I've seen my mom take a ton of these at once. They don't do anything."

He washed them down with the last bit of his drink.

Silas

Silas's head felt like someone was inside his skull pounding with a hammer, trying to pound their way out through his bone. He climbed out of bed and stood up; he had to sit back down because the room was spinning. He looked for Chloe, but didn't see her anywhere. He steadied himself against the wall as he made his way to the bathroom. He felt the humidity of the room as he opened the door. He saw that the bathtub curtain had been pulled shut. "Chloe, are you in there?" he asked. No response. He gripped the edge of the curtain and slowly pulled it away. He saw her there, lying naked in the tub. He reached down for her hand. "Chloe! Chloe!" he yelled and began slapping her hand, trying to wake her up. He noticed that her eyes were shut. He stepped back. "I'll call 911," he said and hurried to the motel phone. He picked it up. Nothing. It was dead. "Fuck!" he yelled.

He stumbled toward the door, opened it and ran out into the rain, into the parking lot. "Someone call an ambulance!" he slurred and began banging on motel doors as he splashed along the sidewalk.

"Someone, please call an ambulance. Call an ambulance! For my girlfriend. She's in room 137."

The next thing he knew, squad cars were pulling up. Their blue lights reflecting off of the white motel walls and the wet blacktop. "Room 137," Silas exhaled and pointed toward the yellow glow of the open door. He was then ushered off to an ambulance.

Silas

"He hasn't been awake yet," a nurse said as she gently squeezed Silas's shoulder. "Excuse me," she said. "There's someone here to speak with you." Silas thought she sounded like an angel. He opened his eyes just as she was stepping out of the room.

"How do you feel?" a woman asked. Silas didn't recognize her. "You had quite a bit of alcohol in your system when you came into the ER last night." She flipped through a chart, "And sleeping pills?"

"I'm okay," Silas said. He sat up on his elbows and squinted. He absorbed the hospital room's fluorescent lights and pastel greens.

"I'm Gail. I'm the hospital social worker. I need to ask you a few questions," she said, and flipped to another page of the chart. Silas thought her voice was comforting, like butterscotch. She sat down in the chair beside the bed. Suddenly everything came rushing back to Silas.

"Is Chloe okay?" Silas asked.

"That's her name? Chloe?"

"Yeah," Silas said. "Where is she? Can I see her?"

"Can you tell me her last name?"

"Chloe Smith," Silas said.

"And what's your name?"

"My name is Silas."

"Silas what?"

"Silas Carlson."

"What's your relation to Chloe?"

"She's my girlfriend. Is she okay?"

"Silas." the woman said. She leaned over and placed her hand on Silas's shoulder.

"What happened? What's wrong?" he asked, panicked.

"Let's focus on getting you in touch with your parents first."

The Hospital

Silas sat in the hospital bed watching TV. He thought about changing from the hospital gown into his regular clothes, but decided against it, thinking that the hospital garb might generate a little more sympathy from his mom and dad. The nurse told him that they both had arrived, but that the social worker had wanted to speak to them both, together, before they spoke to Silas. He turned the TV down; he thought he could hear them discussing something in hushed voices in the hall. Then the door opened; the sound startled him. The social worker walked in first, Silas's dad and mom filed in behind her.

Silas's mom ran over and threw her arms around him. His dad stood next to his bed with his hands in his pockets, observing everything. He nodded his head in acknowledgement. "How are you?" his father asked.

"I'm okay," Silas said as his mom kissed his cheek.

"Well," his dad said slowly, "get your stuff together. We're going to your mom's place to pack up your stuff, and then you're coming to stay with me in Minnesota for a while." Silas looked to his mother for confirmation. She nodded her head and ran her fingers through his hair.

"We thought it'd be best if you had a change of scenery for a bit," she said. "I hope you understand."

"I'll be away from my friends?" Silas asked.

"Yup," his father said.

"Will I be able to come back to see Mom? How long will I be gone?"

"Buddy, you messed up, plain and simple," his dad said. "I've got a lawyer lined up for you down here. You're probably going to have to come back to appear in court, and of course you'll be able to visit your mom, but that'll be on down the road, after we've reestablished some trust. Hitting a girl with your car and then disappearing afterward with this Chloe girl; it's so irresponsible. We think it's best if you live with me, with a little more structure." Silas saw his mom frown, but she remained quiet, as if it had already been decided, as if her hands were tied by the circumstances.

"What about Chloe? What's happened to her?" Silas asked. His mom broke down in tears. "She's dead?" Silas asked.

"Yes, honey," his mom said, looking him in the eyes. "She didn't make it."

"Why? How? Did she miscarry?" Silas asked after a deep sob took his breath away. He watched through his tears as the adults in the room froze and looked to each other for help unfolding the truth for Silas.

"Honey," his mom said, grabbing his hand with both of hers, "she overdosed on sleeping pills and alcohol."

"But I saw blood," Silas said, looking at his mom and then the social worker.

"To be quite honest with you, because of confidentiality and the fact that Chloe was a minor, I can't really talk about it," the social worker said. "I'm sorry," she said and stepped behind Silas's parents to the back of the room.

"It was the police who told me," Silas's mom said.

"Will I be able to go to her funeral before we go?" Silas asked.

"From what I've been able to gather, her family doesn't want to have too much to do with you."

"What do you mean?"

"I mean the state trooper that came to visit your mother said that they've asked that we not contact them, and by *we*, I mean you."

"But, I didn't get to say goodbye." Silas collapsed into his mother and sobbed.

The Long Drive to Minnesota

The dark interior of his father's car was quiet except for the scratchings of the voices on the AM radio. The leather seats and trim were variant dark grays. The fall leaves blurred past the car window; vibrant oranges, deep reds, and brilliant yellows streaked across Silas's view.

"Dad."

"Yeah."

"She haunts me sometimes," Silas said, his forehead pressed against the passenger window, his breath fogging it with every word that escaped his lips.

"What's that?" his dad asked. He turned off the talk radio that filled the silent spaces packed tight between them.

"Chloe. She haunts me," Silas said.

"How's that?" his dad asked.

"When I sleep, she comes and wakes me up," Silas said, making circles with his finger in his breath fog clinging to the window.

"You're dreaming about her?" his dad asked. He looked over at Silas and then back to the road.

"It's like she's there next to me," Silas said.

"But she's not. It's just a dream," his dad said. "You know that, right?"

"She comes to me at night and cries. It's so loud that it wakes me up." Silas stared out the window. "She wants me to come with her, to help her figure out where she's going. She's so scared. I can hear it in her voice."

"Silas, you know that's just a bad dream, right? You know that, don't you?" Again, he looked at Silas and then back to the road. "You're not thinking about suicide or anything like that, are you? I need to know." The panic in his voice surprised Silas.

"No, Dad, I'm not. I know I can't help her," Silas said.

"We'll get you some help, some counseling, when we get back to Minnesota," his dad said, more to himself than to Silas.

"Dad, I don't need counseling. I'm fine," Silas said as he continued to make designs on the window.

Silence.

"You know what?" his dad asked.

"What?"

"I have no idea what I'm doing. I don't know what I should say here. There's no parenting manual explaining how to help your son through…" He stopped. "Hell, I don't even know how to explain what you've been through." He glanced over at Silas. "What's so funny? Why are you smiling?"

"I'm smiling because I have no idea how to explain it either. I don't even know where I'd begin."

"That's where I think counseling could do you some good. You know, help you make sense of it all."

Silas snorted.

"What? Why's that funny?" his dad asked.

"What if it's not supposed to make sense? What if it's so messed up that it doesn't make any sense at all, and that's just the way it is?" Silas could tell by his father's silence that this was something he hadn't considered.

"That's a thought," his father finally said. "I just want to be sure you've learned something from this, you know? I wanna be able to trust you. But..."

"I know," Silas said and leaned back in the seat. "I know."

Silence.

Silas watched his dad as he drove and thought he heard his dad whisper, "What if?" as if he were replaying their conversation in his head. "Did you just say, what if?" Silas asked.

"I don't know. Maybe. I was thinking, what if we just figure this out together? What if we just take it one day at a time?"

"Yeah. Sure. I'm good with that," Silas said. "I can do that." He leaned forward and clicked the radio back on. He changed the station from his father's talk radio to music that he liked, something more upbeat.

For more information on Kill the Middle Man Press, please send an email to:

killthemiddlemanpress@gmail.com

For more information on Joe Dolsen check out:

Joedolsen.blogspot.com